RUNT
FARM

THE
GARDEN

Runt Farm

Clovis Escapes!

Amanda Lorenzo

Illustrations by

Mark Evan Walker

BOOKTI
MOOKTI
PRESS

SEATTLE, WASHINGTON

Contents

Cousin Clovis

Tooth sat in the kitchen, reading a letter. She did not look happy. "Dear me, Cletus," she said, "it's from Clovis."

"Delivered by Chipmunk Mail, I see," replied Cletus, eyeing the teeth marks at the edge of the envelope. "They certainly have an ingenious way about them."

"Yes. I can't imagine how they get in and out of NAARF without being detected, bless their little hearts." She read on. Suddenly she gasped, closed her eyes, then took a deep breath.

"Well, out with it, my dear!" demanded Cletus. "What does Cousin Clovis have to say?"

"This is dreadful!" exclaimed Tooth. "I dare say I knew this day would come. We never should have left her behind, Cletus. Just look!" She shoved the letter under his nose.

"*Hmm*," Cletus read on. "Changed her meds, took away her canvasses and paints. Why, this is outrageous! We must do something." He pulled his cap down hard. This was something Cletus did only when a situation called for drastic action. It was his way of preparing himself for whatever might come next.

Tooth folded the letter and stuffed it in the pocket of her apron. She began fussing about, straightening the jars on the spice rack.

"Dear Clovis had been doing so well," she lamented. "Living at NAARF is a terrible vexation by any standards, but she had so valiantly adapted to the place. It did seem as though she was going to be all right on her own. Oh Cletus, she must be beside herself! No paints, and strange meds. I just can't imagine . . ."

Cletus stood up tall. "I'll fire up the Wicker Crane and go at once," he said.

"But Cletus, what about your brace?" Tooth objected. She laid her hand on his arm. "You'd never get past the metal detectors. Surely you remember that ghastly racket when we escaped."

Tooth gazed intently out the window, as if seeing through the forest, past the giant doors of NAARF, all the way to Clovis's cage perched high atop the others. She sighed deeply.

"So much easier to break out of NAARF than to get back in. . . . And getting out was no picnic, I dare say!" Tooth bit her lip and ran a sink full of sudsy water. Then she took up a plate and sponge and began thinking. She always thought more clearly while doing dishes.

"Well, you're right about that, Tooth," said Cletus, rubbing his leg appreciatively. "But I hope you're not planning to go back there yourself. I don't mean to be rude, you know, but even at your top speed, I fear it's unlikely you'd get through . . . ." Tooth gave Cletus a stern look that made the words evaporate in his

mouth. Tooth was not as
fast as she used to be, it
was true. But saying so
just then wasn't especially
helpful.

Suddenly two noses
poked around the doorway.

"Me! I want to go,"
Beatrice interrupted. Her whiskers twitched at
the notion of an adventure. "Where we goin'?
To market? I've always wanted to go to market!
Can we, can we, can we go to market?"

"You don't even know what the market is!"
said Blossom.

"Do so!" said Beatrice, giving him a tiny
nudge.

"Do not," said Blossom, nudging her back.

"My dears, the destination is far more

dangerous than even the market," said Tooth. "We must go to NAARF to retrieve my Cousin Clovis." Tooth shook her head in dismay.

"Well okay then! Let's go! Let's get Cousin Clovis!" cried Beatrice, standing at attention.

"I'm afraid that's impossible," Tooth fretted, as she dried the cups and saucers. "It's no place for young ones, certainly."

Cletus broke in. "But look there . . .

Beatrice is just the right size for the job. Quite agile, too, and the bravest bunny we know." He winked at Beatrice who smiled and stood even taller.

"*I'm* brave, too!" protested Blossom.

"And no doubt of it, sir!" Cletus quickly agreed. "But someone's got to stay here and help me get things set up for our guest." Blossom nodded. He saw the logic in this.

Beatrice pleaded, "*Pleeease*, Auntie Tooth. . . . Please let me go with you!"

Tooth ignored the whining. The first order of business was to consult with Cletus about her cousin's living quarters. The poor thing had been through so much already! It would surely help to have a nice place of her own to come home to.

"Cousin Clovis will need a proper room,

Cletus," said Tooth. "You know how she is about wide open spaces. A studio in the loft, I think . . . where the light is good."

"And a skylight!" Cletus added as the project took shape in his mind. "Yes, I can do that. Blossom, I'll need your help," he said.

"Oh boy!" cried Blossom. "I'll get some wood."

Cletus stopped him. "Hold up now, son. First we'll have to build a lift. I can't get up and down the ladder like you can, you know!" Blossom beamed.

"What's up? Can we help with something?" asked Kitten, as he and The Peep joined the others in the kitchen.

"Sure can," said Cletus. "Come with me to the shop, and I'll fill you in."

At last Tooth turned to Beatrice. "Dear,

I'm going to make some food to take along. You fetch a grandma quilt and a flashlight. We'll leave at dark."

"Hurray!" cried Beatrice. "I'll be a big help, you'll see!"

"Why, I've no doubt of that in the least," said Tooth. She busied herself collecting the provisions for their journey. Beatrice hopped off, eager to do her part.

"Oh, I'm a flashing quilter, and a merry

one am I!" the bunny sang, making up goofy verses as she gathered up the quilt and found the flashlight. Beatrice clicked the flashlight on and off on a few times, just to be sure it still worked. Quilts and flashlights belong together, she thought. You have to have both if you want to read or play games at night without waking anybody up.

It wasn't long before Beatrice and Tooth piled the necessary items into the Wicker Crane. Tooth sat at the helm, steering them toward NAARF. Beatrice studied the blueprints closely, as they zoomed away from Runt Farm.

"Now remember," Tooth said, "Clovis will be wearing a red beret." After a bit, Tooth asked, "Have you memorized the floor plan?" Being a bunny of uncommon capacity, Beatrice had.

"Yes, I know the floor plan, but how will I get in the front door?" Beatrice frowned.

"Listen carefully, dear," said Tooth. "The shift changes at 11 o'clock. You'll have to sneak

in behind the new guard as he comes on duty."

"That's called *tailgating*," said Beatrice. She wasn't exactly sure where she'd heard the term, but it didn't matter. Hopping along behind someone without them seeing you was a welcome chance to develop good sneaking skills. "Betcha I'll be good at that!" she said.

"I expect you will, dear," said Tooth gravely, "but you must also stay extremely alert. NAARF is a tricky place for small animals . . ." Her voice trailed off.

Beatrice assumed a fearsome pose. "I can be tricky, too, if I want to!" she exclaimed, making a few quick moves with her paws to back it up. "I'm going to take this Wicker Crane hook right up to the top floor, put it on Clovis's cage, and give a great big yank. And nobody'd better try and stop me, either!" she blustered.

"Yes indeed, that's the plan. And then I'll run the winch just a little bit to bend the bars so Cousin Clovis can get out." Tooth sighed. She hoped the rescue plan would take shape just that easily, but secretly she wondered.

"Uh huh," said Beatrice, glancing at the floor plan. "And then Clovis and I will ride the hook *all* the way back to the *door*." She paused a moment, imagining all of it.

Beatrice pulled on Tooth's apron. "And then how do we get back out?" she asked.

Tooth bit her lip. Just then she cut the engine and rolled the Wicker Crane to a stop.

They were now in the bushes near the front door of the NAARF lab.

"Well dear, I'm afraid I haven't worked out that part just yet. We'll just have to see how things develop as we go along."

Beatrice's eyes grew wide.

"Now don't you worry, dear," Tooth reassured her. "You just signal me with your flashlight when you reach the lobby. I'll think of something."

Beatrice gathered all her bravery into her belly. Then she stomped her feet for extra confidence.

"Okay, here I go," she said. She grabbed hold of the hook and started off.

Bunny on the Run

Beatrice wound her way through the halls and walls of NAARF. Soon she had arrived at the row of cages, stacked several high. Crouched far back in the penthouse cage was a scrawny mouse, shivering all over—and sure enough, she was wearing a red beret! Gosh, thought Beatrice, Clovis doesn't look so good.

Gently Beatrice tapped on the cage.

"Hi there, Clovis," said Beatrice with her friendliest smile. "You don't know me, but I'm Beatrice. Cletus and Tooth sent me to get you out of here."

Clovis clutched at the grey blanket lining her cage. "*Eeep!*" she cried feebly.

This is going to be tough, thought Beatrice. She whispered to Clovis in a soothing voice. "Please, Clovis, try to . . . you have to be as quiet as . . . as a . . . just be really quiet, okay?"

Beatrice quickly put the hook in place and

gave the line a sharp tug.
As soon as Tooth felt
the tension at her end,
she pulled the winch
lever. But to her dismay,
it wouldn't stop!

"Oh dear, oh dear, oh dear!" cried Tooth,
watching helplessly as the winch whined and
the line went tight.

Back inside NAARF, the entire wall of
cages came crashing down. Beatrice clung to
Clovis's cage with all her might, as row upon
row of the tiny wire apartments toppled into
a heap. Animals of all kinds scampered out
everywhere. And among them were . . . the
enemy.

"Yikes!" cried Beatrice, quivering. "Tooth
didn't tell me there would be *weasels!*"

"*Eeeep!*" whimpered Clovis. She slipped through the bent bars and joined Beatrice on top of the cage.

"Clovis! Let's get you out of here," Beatrice cried. But suddenly the crane hook, still attached to Clovis's cage, began dragging them up, up, and up the side of the wall! Beatrice looked down. A weasel was winding his way up and around the bottom of the cage, hoping for a two-course meal of mouse and rabbit. Clovis clutched at Beatrice in terror.

"*Eeep!*" Clovis wailed.

Just then Beatrice spotted an open ventilator shaft at the top of the wall. And without even thinking, the little bunny grabbed Clovis's paw and made the biggest leap of

her life. *Snap!*
The hook
popped through
the bars. Weasel
and all, the cage went
hurtling to the floor of
the NAARF lab.

"Whew, that was a close one!" sighed
Beatrice. "But gosh, Clovis, we were supposed
to ride the hook back to Tooth. Now it's gone,
and I don't know how to get back to the door."

Stunned as she was by the toppling of
her living quarters, Clovis couldn't speak.
Clutching her beret, she simply pointed down
the ventilation shaft.

"*Eeep!*" she managed. Beatrice glanced over.

"This way?" Beatrice asked. Clovis nodded.
"Okay then, let's go!" she said.

They made their way down the shaft as
quickly as they could. It was clear going until
they heard a whirring sound ahead. As they
ran, the sound grew louder. Soon they were
facing the blades of a gigantic fan, whirling
dangerously fast. Beatrice and Clovis stopped in
their tracks.

"*Eeep*," Clovis
objected feebly.
"It's all
right," urged
Beatrice. "See,
that blade? It
has a chunk
missing. We just
have to time it right to
get through. You can do it. See, just count one .
. . two . . . three . . . and then *run!*" Clovis closed

her eyes and winced.

"Go on, Clovis! Tooth's waiting!" Beatrice cried. Then, with one long and warrior-like *eeeeeep*, Cousin Clovis scampered toward the fan—but stopped herself just short of the blades.

"Whoa there, Clovis! You gave me a scare!" shouted Beatrice. "We may have to try this another way. And I sure hope you get your words back. Right now you sound kinda like The Peep."

"*Peeep?*" said Clovis. Beatrice tried not to roll her eyes.

"I'm tellin' you," said Beatrice, "we've gotta get going. Here, I'll help you." Beatrice gathered up Cousin Clovis and her beret. She tucked the quivering mouse under her arm like a football and prepared to make a headlong run for the fan.

"One . . . two . . . three . . . Here I *go!*" cried Beatrice, as she raced through the blades and out onto the laboratory rooftop.

In the night air, shrill sirens were blaring. Red and yellow lights flashed atop every

building in the NAARF complex. Beatrice heard the sound of voices, but they were soon drowned out by the loud whirr of helicopter blades. Squinting over the edge of the roof, Beatrice caught sight of a tiny, aproned figure standing next to a not-much-larger contraption made of wicker.

"Look, Clovis!" cried Beatrice. "There's Tooth and the Wicker Crane, but it's really a long way down." She began calling, "Tooth, Tooth, we're up here. *Help!*"

Encouraged by the sight of her Cousin Tooth, Clovis motioned to a nearby drainhole. "*Eeep, eeep,*" she offered.

"*Shhh!*" warned Beatrice. "They'll hear you." But that didn't stop Clovis. She threw herself at the pipe as she tugged hard on Beatrice's fur, so hard that both bunny and

mouse went hurtling down the drainpipe one after the other in a tumbling mass of ears, feet, and whiskers.

"*Eeew*," complained Beatrice, wiping at her fur. "That was slimy."

"But effective, nevertheless!" cried Tooth joyfully. "My goodness, but it's splendid to see you both! I was so worried when the hook returned without you." She embraced Cousin Clovis tenderly.

"Yep, we made it, no problem," Beatrice bragged. "And Tooth, there were weasels and sirens and . . ."

"Quickly now, Beatrice dear," Tooth broke in. "We must leave at once."

"*Eeep!*" agreed Clovis.

"Uh huh!" said Beatrice.

Back at Runt Farm, Cletus and the others had prepared a lovely new room just for Clovis, in a corner of the barn loft. It was high up, which Clovis was used to. But it was safe and quiet, which she wasn't used to. At least not yet. They all promised Tooth they would watch out for Cousin Clovis until she got settled.

On their way to bed, Beatrice told Blossom about the weasel, and Blossom showed Beatrice the new lift platform. And down in the kitchen, Cletus and Tooth sat at the table with cups of tea, a grandma quilt pulled close around them. In warm tones, the two mice talked long into the night.

Cletus and the Big Cheese

A loud knocking came at the barn door.
"Special delivery for C. Maus! Special delivery!"

"Goodness gracious, what a racket!"
exclaimed Tooth as she stepped into the
sunlight. Two official-looking chipmunks stood
before her, guarding a heavy box wrapped in
brown paper and tied with twine.

"Oh dear me, that's quite a package! But
I'm sorry to say you've come to the wrong
address. We have no C. Maus at Runt Farm."

"Says right here, lady: C. Maus, Runt

Farm," said the chipmunk wearily, puffing out his cheeks.

"Yeah," added his assistant, "we don't make mistakes, ya know."

Tooth took a deep breath and remembered that she was a patient mouse. But before she had a chance to correct the mistaken munks, Cletus strolled out of the barn.

"Well, this is grand indeed. I see it has arrived. A great day, truly!" He patted the package, checking to be sure it wasn't damaged.

"Cletus, I . . . this is . . . would you kindly explain?" Tooth blustered. At times like these, she never seemed to be able to find the words she wanted.

"No need to worry, dear Tooth," he mumbled, as he signed for the package.

"Well, if I *am* at a loss, perhaps it is because I'm faced with a very *big* mystery sitting on our doorstep. Who, may I ask, is C. Maus, and why is his mail being delivered to *us*?" Tooth had never been fond of odd surprises. At least, not this kind.

"All will be revealed," said Cletus as he tipped the chipmunks. He headed back into the barn, calling over his shoulder, "I'll need the Wicker Crane to move this inside."

"Oh, no you don't. Not one more step! Come

back here this minute and enlighten me, sir."

Reluctantly, Cletus returned and stood by the mystery package. "Well, I was hoping to surprise you," he said, "and if we open it out here it could spoil."

Cletus paused for dramatic effect. This new information did not have a calming effect on Tooth. She began tapping her foot, and the

look in her eye told Cletus he had better move quickly.

"Just let me get it inside, and we'll open it together," said Cletus. "I'll tell you everything. I promise."

Soon the large box was sitting in the middle of the cool barn. The whole family gathered around.

"Wow," said Blossom, "that's one whopper of a box, Cletus. What's in it?"

"Is it for me?" Beatrice pushed forward and squinted at the label. "Oh," she said. Her ears drooped a bit. "The name starts with a

C like *Cletus*, not a *B* like *Beatrice*." She paused. "I know my letters up through G, H, and I," she said, a fact which made her feel better.

"Not *B* for *Blossom*, either," the squirrel added glumly.

"Guess that rules out Kitten and The Peep, too, then," said Kitten to his little yellow buddy.

"*C* as in *Cletus*?" Tooth repeated suspiciously.

"Yes, it's me. Or rather it's my pseudonym. A mix, you know. *C* being my first initial, of

course. And the *Maus* is German for *mouse*.
Couldn't use *Cletus Mouse*. Too obvious.
NAARF would have caught wind of that right
off," Cletus rambled.

"NAARF!" Tooth had now reached the end
of her patience.

Cletus began chewing nervously on the
twine that was holding the package together.
"Per-whaps uf we jus . . . opun mit," he
sputtered, pulling hard with his teeth. *Twang!*
The twine gave way. The box fell open to reveal
an enormous wheel-shaped object encased in
bright red wax.

"Look," said Cletus, "it's cheese, see?" Now
Tooth would understand.

"Tooth, just think, you can make cheese
soufflés, cheese toast, cheese anything, really!
Perhaps for dessert tonight, your famous

cheesecake . . ." he suggested.

"*Peep, peep, peep!*" The Peep added, requesting his favorite: potatoes au gratin.

"Cletus," said Tooth, "cheesecake is made with *cream* cheese. This is a wheel of cheddar."

"I wouldn't mind it with cheddar, though," he said. "We all love what you do with cheese, dear." He gave Tooth his most charming smile. She sighed.

While the family admired the big cheese, Tooth tore open the envelope attached to the package. She read, "Thank you for your order from The Cheese Castle . . . credit is approved . . . monthly payments . . . year of . . . Oh dear me!" Tooth sat down and began fanning herself with the letter.

"What is it, dear?" asked Cletus, giving her shoulder an affectionate pat.

"Cletus." Tooth took a deep breath. "Cletus, this isn't just one cheese. You've ordered a whole *year* of cheese!" she wailed.

"Better and better! I've outdone myself," he said proudly.

Tooth gathered her wits and began barking orders. "All right everyone, time to go outside and play. Cletus, kindly join me in the kitchen. Right now, all of you, let's go!"

Kitten knew what that meant. He glanced at The Peep sidewise. "Good thing it's not us," he said. The younger animals left as gradually as possible, hoping to catch a word or two on their way out of the barn.

"Cletus, I hardly know where to begin. Whatever were you thinking? How did you manage such a thing? And how in the world are we going to pay for an entire year's worth of cheese?"

"Quite simple, actually," said Cletus. "Nothing to it once you know how. A few numbers here, a new name, an online persona . . ."

"Online persona! What in the world do you mean? We don't even have a computer!" Tooth bustled over to the stove and put on the tea kettle. Definitely time for chamomile tea, she thought. With velvetina root. And a pinch of calming wetherwort . . .

"Not a whole computer, to be sure, just a few components. A bit tricky getting a wireless connection out here, but nothing I couldn't handle. As for payments, that's no problem at all. I charged the cheese to the Chairman of the Board at NAARF. So you see, everything is fine!"

Tooth gasped. "Cletus, my deluded dear, everything is *far* from fine." She held up her paw and began to count off each item. "One: you stole someone's identity. Two: you made a fraudulent order under a false name. And three: you had the evidence of your crime delivered *right to our door!*"

Cletus shifted impatiently. "Well, when you put it that way, then of course it sounds bad. But think, dear! It's . . . *cheese!*" He lingered over the flavorful word, and his eyes opened wide. In all other respects, Cletus was a mouse of extraordinary intelligence. Again and again his abilities had astonished the scientists at NAARF. Yet when it came to the matter of cheese, reason failed him entirely.

"And what do you think will happen when the Chairman discovers he's a member of the Cheese-A-Month Club?"

Cletus hung his head. "I guess I didn't see it very clearly. It was chee . . ."

"Yes, I know it was cheese," said Tooth, standing her ground. "Really, I don't understand what comes over you when this subject comes up. It's becoming quite a problem. In fact I'd say it's . . . *ingravescent!*"

"Please don't say that," moped Cletus. "It's not getting worse. I've always felt this way about cheese. And it was such a great opportunity."

Tooth shook her head. "Well, we certainly have our share of trouble now, sir," she said. "We'll have to call a family meeting. Decisions must be made, and plans . . . strategies," she added. "I know this will be difficult for you, but you must be honest with the young ones. We're responsible for their education, Cletus. We can't have them thinking identity theft is a life skill!"

"You're right, of course. I've made quite a muddle of this." Cletus took out his handkerchief and blew his nose loudly.

She patted his shoulder. "Tea?"

That night the family gathered to hear the story of the big cheese. That is, everyone

except Clovis, who still wouldn't come down
from the loft. When Cletus had finished
confessing his crime, he asked their help and

forgiveness.

Kitten went first. "That's okay, Cletus. You've saved our behinds plenty of times! Sure we're gonna help. Right, Peep?" The Peep waddled over and nuzzled the big mouse. A teary-eyed Cletus wrapped his arm around the little duck.

"I usually have great ideas, but this wasn't one of them," he admitted. "And now that it's done, I'm not sure how to fix it."

Beatrice piped up, "Can't we just send the dumb old cheese back where it came from?"

"No, we can't," said Tooth. "It's perishable and can't be returned. Even if we did send it back, the Chairman would see a suspicious credit on his account."

"Maybe he doesn't look that closely at his bills," offered Kitten.

"We can't count on that, dear," Tooth said firmly. "And as we've already discussed, it is not right to steal. We need an *honest* solution."

Blossom had been sitting with his head in his paws, listening. "Hey," he said, brightening. "Why don't we just write a letter to NAARF and tell them it was all a big mistake?"

"Are you *kidding?*" Beatrice shouted. "You've never been there! Everything about that place is . . . is . . . it's *naarfy*, that's what it is. There's cages and weasels. You can't trust NAARF!"

"Yeah, well . . . see? I told you there's stuff out there you can't trust," Blossom countered.

No one noticed when The Peep slipped out of the kitchen. They all took turns coming up with solutions, but each new plan was flawed. What to do? At last they sat in silence. They had no money to pay for the cheese.

To their surprise, the duckling returned pushing a tiny wheelbarrow. They were even more surprised to see what was inside. Shiny stacks of dimes and nickels.

"Whoa, dude! Where'd all this come from?" asked Kitten. And The Peep proceeded to explain.

"No way!" said Blossom when The Peep had finished.

"Unbelievable," said Tooth.

"Ingenious!" said Cletus. "Should have thought of it myself."

Beatrice was breathless. "You've been picking corn from the kitchen garden?"

"And selling it to a pig family over in Muddy Meadow?" Blossom sputtered. "Wow, how much have you got?"

The Peep held up his little wings: *This much.*

The family heaved a collective sigh. However much that was, they knew it wasn't enough to pay for even one wheel of cheese, much less a whole year's worth.

That night's dinner was especially quiet. No one dared ask why a certain delicacy wasn't on the menu. They all knew that Tooth would sooner let the cheese go green with mold than serve up a single stolen mouthful. This saddened Cletus a great deal. He spent the evening hours walking around his prize, sniffing it here and patting it there, until Tooth told him to go to bed.

"We need to be sharp in the morning," she said. "We still have to figure this out."

The next day dawned cold. A brisk wind blew across Puddlefoot Pond and into the barn. "Fall's coming on," Tooth said, as the family gathered for breakfast.

Cletus brightened, adding, "Oh, the cold will help to preserve the chee . . ." But he stopped short when he saw the pained expressions on their faces.

"I'll just have to turn myself in to NAARF and protect you all. Say it was just me. I can always go back to researching improvements to the electron micro . . ." His brave proposition was met with a chorus of objections.

Kitten gave Cletus a look. "Man, that is the most half-baked thing you ever said."

At that, Blossom did a flip right in the kitchen. "That's it!" he

hollered. "That's what we can do!"

"Not following you, bro," said Kitten. "What are we gonna do?"

"*Bake!*" Blossom said, wide-eyed. "We can . . . I mean, Tooth can bake stuff and we can sell it." His tail twitched feverishly. "The Peep already knows how to sell, and Tooth can make anything!"

Tooth smiled. Not a bad idea, she thought.

Blossom's vision set off a flurry of chatter around the breakfast table. Everyone had a suggestion about what Tooth should bake. Tooth ran over to her recipe books and began pulling out jars of ingredients.

"I want us to make yummy cookies and call them Beatrice Buttons," suggested You-Know-Who.

"Buttons are boring," said Blossom. "We

should make Braided Blossoms. They could be shaped like flowers with cheesy centers. That'd be cute!"

Kitten suggested Kippered Kitten Snacks, and they all shot him a look. It was agreed that they couldn't call the product Peep Peep Peep, either.

Cletus stood up. "I'd like to propose that we have a brand name: Toothsome Treats, in honor of our dear Tooth. And the first product can be called . . . Cheesy Puffers!

"Yeah!" everyone cheered. "Cheesy Puffers!"

The name had a roll-off-the-tongue ring to it, even if none of them knew exactly what a cheesy puffer was. Certainly they had plenty of the main ingredient on hand. Before long, Tooth came up with a cheesefully crunchy recipe that pleased everyone.

In a few days Runt Farm was transformed into a Cheesy Puffer factory. Cletus invented a conveyor baking system. Kitten and The Peep set up a distribution network. Tooth let Cletus go online to open a Pay-Your-Pal account so he could pay for the year's worth of cheese. And they sent a note to The Cheese Castle to switch the bill so the charges wouldn't go to the Chairman's credit card.

Before long every chipmunk, hoot owl, and gopher in the neighborhood was standing in line to take home a package of Toothsome Treats. Money came in, and the cheese bill got paid right on time. Tooth even managed to set aside savings for a rainy day. Just like Grandma Nellie, Tooth had always known when a rainy day was coming. But she kept that thought to herself.

And the best part? Cheese was now on the menu for good, and this made Cletus very happy indeed. He never tired of cheese and anything that went with it. "Everything goes with cheese!" he was often heard to say. Every night as he tucked the youngsters into their beds, he sang them a cheesy little ditty that went like this:

Cheese it is that soothes the soul.
Creamy smooth to fill the bowl.
Go to sleepy, cheesy heads.
Now you know it's time for bed.

Parts of the song didn't make much sense, but no one seemed to mind. Beatrice in particular didn't think her head was cheesy. But she kept that thought to herself.

Family is a Verb

Clovis Goes Blue

Beatrice, Tooth, and Blossom were making lunch in the kitchen.

"When is Clovis going to get better?" Beatrice asked.

Tooth said, "I don't know, dear, we'll just have to give her more time. You take this tray up and see if she'll eat a little something. Clovis seems to like it when you visit. I'm going out now to look for some herbs that may help."

"Yeah, she needs a poultice or something,"

said Blossom. "Can I help you look?"

"Certainly, dear. Bring your bag along, and we'll see what we can find."

In the days since her escape from NAARF, everyone at Runt Farm had tried to think of ways to help Clovis. Blossom had brought an assortment of nuts and piled them up by her door. *Everyone likes nuts*, he thought.

Tooth cooked special things for dinner, like cheesy potatoes and corn on the cob, hoping Clovis would come down and eat with the family. Cletus stretched canvases over wooden frames and left them stacked in the loft in case Clovis felt inspired to paint.

The Peep sang soft little songs near Clovis's door, and Kitten offered her a ride in the Reed Basket.

Beatrice even gave Clovis her blue peewee

marble.

But nothing worked. Clovis sat in her loft room alone. She didn't come out to eat, or to play with Beatrice and Blossom when they invited her. Clovis didn't paint, either. For days on end, her brushes sat in a neat row along the windowsill, untouched. She had even hung her tattered NAARF blanket over the big window to block out the light.

After leaving the lunch tray for Clovis, Beatrice climbed back down from the loft and headed right to Cletus's shop. "I left Cousin Clovis some lunch, but I bet she doesn't eat it. I think she's got a rexia or something."

"Well, at least she's stopped saying *eeep*," said Cletus. "She certainly has been blue."

"I've done all the same things you and Tooth did when I first came to Runt Farm:

grandma quilts, poultices, hugs, warm soup. But Clovis doesn't care about any of those things." Beatrice sighed.

"Yes," said Cletus. "When cheesy potatoes didn't do the trick, I was sure this was going to be a tough case. Let's go take a little drive and see what we can find that might help." Cletus rubbed his tummy, thinking of cheesy potatoes.

"Off we go!" he said, as they rumbled out of the barn in the rickety Wicker Crane. When they rounded the corner by Picnic Hill, Cletus said, "Came past here the other day. Pretty sure I saw something that needed further investigation."

"What, Uncle Cletus?" asked young Beatrice.

"Look right there," Cletus pointed. "What do you see?"

"Blueberries!" cried the bunny. Beatrice loved blueberries. They reminded her of her favorite marble: the blue peewee. "Do you think Clovis will like them?" she asked.

"Well, let's gather up a batch, and we'll just see about that, shall we?" said Cletus as he hopped out. He let down the hook and attached a big net to it. Beatrice wandered further into the blueberry thicket.

"Cletus, wow!" she called. "Look at this one!" Cletus waded into the patch. He saw Beatrice jumping up and down near a giant bush. She was pointing at an enormous blue fruit overhead.

"That's a record-breaker all right! Don't know as I've ever seen one quite that size. Must be half again as tall as you are, my dear!"

Beatrice beamed. "Can we get it, Uncle

Cletus, can we, please?" she pleaded as she hopped in place. "Do you think you could get it down?"

"Why sure, I can do that," said Cletus. True to his word, he rigged the net, dropped it neatly over the big berry, and winched it down to the ground. "Let's get a few of the smaller ones, too," he added.

"Yes, we'll need a bunch. And I have special plans for that one," said Beatrice, pointing to the giant fruit.

"Is that so?" asked Cletus, raising an eyebrow.

Beatrice hurried to explain. "Yes, I have big idea and . . . and . . ."

"Let me guess: it requires an extra-large

blueberry," Cletus chuckled.

"Right!" smiled Beatrice. "Uncle Cletus, you are so smart."

"All right then, let's haul our catch back home and show it off," said Cletus. "Success loves company, you know."

When Cletus and Beatrice arrived at the barn, Blossom and Tooth were in the kitchen cleaning and sorting herbs. On the stove sat a hefty pot, steaming away.

Huffing and puffing, Beatrice rolled her prize through the doorway. "Look, just look what we found!"

Blossom's eyes got big. "Cool, Bea. We could make a pie. Lots of pies," he said, reaching out to touch it.

"No!" said Beatrice, guarding the berry with both paws. "This one's for Clovis. I'm taking it to her right now."

"Don't worry, son," Cletus broke in. "We have plenty more for pie."

Cheered by this news, Blossom offered to help Beatrice find a serving bowl. Tooth had just the thing. Turning the bowl on its side, they rolled the giant berry in.

"Cream!" cried Beatrice. "We'll need some cream, too. That will make it extra special," she explained. Tooth offered to do the pouring.

"Can you two manage that all right?" Tooth asked, as squirrel and bunny squared off around the bowl to get a good grip.

"Sure, we can do it," said Blossom, panting.

He and Beatrice raised the bowl and walked it out to the lift. Hardly any cream was lost along the way.

"Okay, now help me get this up here," bossed Beatrice, intent on her plan. "Then you go knock on the door, and I'll take it in to Clovis!"

As bowl and bunny went up on the lift, Blossom scampered to the top of the ladder. He arrived just in time to meet Beatrice and the berry. Blossom gave a sharp tap-tap-tap, and Beatrice ushered the dessert through Clovis's door.

Clovis saw a huge ball of blue coming toward her in a red bowl. A milky substance seemed to be leaking from its skin.

"*Eeep!*" cried Clovis, as she shrank back on her bed. Then Beatrice set the bowl on the table and peeked out from behind it.

"Look, I brought you Blueberry and Cream. It's my new favorite!" said Beatrice encouragingly.

Clovis stared at the gigantic fruit. She moved closer and sat down to look it over.

"We can share, okay?" said Beatrice. "See, you can eat over there and I'll start over here," she added, taking her place on one side of the table.

The two began to eat. After a bit, Beatrice peeked around. Clovis's whiskers were blue! She glanced down at her own whiskers. Yep. Blue as a berry! Beatrice giggled.

"This is fun," she said. "We're both turning blue!" Clovis didn't say anything. But she kept eating.

Clovis and Beatrice ate and ate until they met . . . in the middle of the berry.

Clovis stopped and stared. A bluish bunny stared back at her.

"I see you, Auntie Clovis!" Beatrice giggled, berry juice dripping from her whiskers.

Clovis gazed at her for a long time without saying anything. Then she ran over to the  window and pulled down the tattered blanket. Light poured into the loft. Clovis ran to the center of the room and took another long look at Beatrice.

"Don't move!" she squeaked.

Beatrice froze in place, amazed.

Clovis scurried over to the pile of canvases, paints, and brushes. She quickly selected what she needed. When the easel was set up, she began to paint. With rapid strokes she transformed the little canvas. A picture began

to emerge . . . a portrait of Beatrice surrounded
by blue.

"Oh, the light, the light! I must finish
before we lose this excellent light," Clovis
chattered as she worked.

"Don't worry," said Beatrice, careful not
to move. "We have lots of light. Cletus put in
'lectricity."

"That's eee-lectricity my dear, and it's nothing compared to the natural light streaming in through this beautiful window. I must thank Cletus for his thoughtfulness in building it. But most of all, Beatrice, I must thank you for being my muse. Now you have rescued me twice."

Then Clovis smiled! And the two of them stepped back to view the finished painting.

"Is that what a muse looks like?" asked Beatrice.

"Yes, I suppose so," replied Clovis.

The young rabbit ran to the edge of the loft and shouted down to the others. "Hey, I'm a muse! Come up and see!"

The whole Runt Farm family came running. They crowded into Clovis's room to see the fresh painting. Clovis and Beatrice got hugs of congratulation all around.

That night Clovis came down to have dinner with the family. Kitten and The Peep scooted over and made room, and Blossom brought out his feather boa for Clovis to try on (but not for keeps). When the blueberry pie was passed around, Clovis and Beatrice just laughed and shook their blue heads.

"We had our dessert first," explained Beatrice, "so we'll just pass. Besides, a muse never eats more than one berry a day."

"Is that so?" grinned Cletus, winking at Tooth.

"Quite so!" chirped Clovis.

And so it was that Blueberry and Cream became an important tradition at Runt Farm. To be served whenever anyone needed food for inspiration.

Peep on a String

"Ah me, how I love these bombilatious days of Indian Summer," Tooth said as the three mice—she, Cletus, and her Cousin Clovis—drove toward Picnic Hill.

"Are you referring to the buzzing of the bees, dear?" asked Cletus. "Or perhaps the humming we've been hearing from Clovis's loft now that she's painting again?" Clovis smiled.

"All of it, I should say," said Tooth. "And this will likely be our last outdoor event before the blustery weather sets in, you know."

"Yes, that reminds me," Cletus said. "I'm preparing the special effects for next month's Halloween extravaganza. Extremely secret, of course. The youngsters should be suitably entertained. Though it's turned out to be a job for no less than eight paws. Might you lend me a bit of assistance with the Tesla coil?"

"Oh dear, I'm much too busy with recipe research and baking plans these days. Clovis, would you like to help Cletus set up a light show?"

"Ah, the light. You know how I love fresh and interesting kinds of light, cousin!" Starry-eyed, Clovis smiled out the window as the Wicker Crane bounced along.

"I'll take that as a yes," said Cletus. He parked his rickety ride next to the oak tree on the top of the hill, and dropped the picnic basket down to the ground. Beatrice and Blossom spread the tablecloth on the grass, then ran off to see Kitten's brand new kite. The Peep stood by, too, watching carefully as Kitten explained how it worked.

"You hold the string like this, see? Then you motor up your hind legs, uh . . . your feet. You run 'til you're going 'bout as fast as you can! And then the kite lifts up in the air. You can do it, buddy. No doubt."

The Peep hopped in an excited circle, warming up. Then he ran to the tree and back again, practicing for speed.

"I want to fly it, too," said Beatrice. "When is it my turn?"

"Me too!" cried Blossom. "Those are my favorite colors! Red and gold and purple!"

"Just a sec, you guys," said Kitten, holding up a paw. "We haven't even put the tail on it yet. And The Peep gets to go first, okay? I promised him."

"Beatrice and Blossom, please come help with the food now!" called Tooth. The two reluctantly left the kite-making lesson and headed over to help Tooth, as she hauled a variety of picnic goodies out of the basket and onto the tablecloth. The young rabbit and squirrel laid out the corn cakes, okra, and fancy olives. Tooth set out a plate of watermelon pickles, crispy cucumbers, and baby-leaf greens.

"This warm potato crisp is just right for a breezy day," said Tooth, arranging the plates. "And there we are!" she announced, standing back to admire the beauty of a meal on the grass.

Beatrice rang the picnic bell to call everyone to eat. Cletus selected an ear of baby corn and was just beginning to enjoy a nibble, when he looked up in alarm. Kitten was running alongside The Peep, who was gripping the kite string. The spool rolled along behind them on the grassy hilltop.

"Oh boys!" Cletus called, "I'm afraid that based on the duck's weight to the coefficient of kite surface area, you're heading for disast . . . !"

But it was too late. A gust of wind had snatched the tiny kite up into the air. And just as Cletus had warned, The Peep went up right along with it. "*Peep, PEEP!*" he exclaimed, flapping madly, still gripping the string.

"Let go! Let go, buddy!" Kitten shouted. He turned and pounced again and again, trying to catch the string.

The spool of string bounced wildly around, and the kite rose higher and higher. As the string played out, the spool raced down the hillside. Blossom, Beatrice, and Kitten ran fast, hoping to grab it and stop the kite from getting away. But before they could reach it, the string ran out and the empty spindle rolled out of sight.

Just then the kite caught a fresh breeze and soared even higher, pulling the tiny yellow duck behind it. Now and then, The Peep's webbed feet ran in midair circles.

"Don't let go now!" Cletus shouted. "Hang on, son!" The Peep thrashed about as the kite flipped this way and that in the wind.

"Oh my," said Cletus. "He's never flown before, you know. At least not from such a height. He may be too frightened to flap his wings properly. This is serious."

"Cletus!" shouted Tooth. "He's headed back toward the barn!" The group abandoned their summer meal and ran for the vehicles. Careening down the hill, they gave chase to the kite and its tiny captive.

High in the air and holding tight, The Peep was having a fine time. He could see the

top of the tree on Picnic Hill. He could see
Tooth and Cletus and Clovis and Kitten driving
along below, while Beatrice and Blossom
pedaled to keep up. The Peep wasn't afraid at
all, until suddenly he saw . . . something! He
let out a flurry of warnings, but his friends were
too far away to hear.

"What's he saying?" Clovis squeaked. "I
can't make it out."

"He's too high up! Poor little fellow must
be terrified," said Cletus.

The Peep flapped his wings furiously, calling
out his dire message. The kite swooped and
soared, then dive-bombed the roof of the barn.

"Oh my ears and whiskers!" cried Tooth.
The wind wrapped the string around the
weathervane, leaving The Peep dangling over the
edge of the roof as the kite settled to the ground.

Still squawking about
what he had seen,
The Peep let go and
fluttered downward,
just as the Reed Basket
and the Wicker Crane
drove up.

The Peep landed right on the hood of the
Wicker Crane.

Now everyone could hear exactly what The
Peep was saying. Clovis's hair stood on end, and
she let out an *eeeeep!* Tooth's eyes sparked with
anger. For a moment no one could move.

Cletus was the first to come to his senses.
He leaped out of the Wicker Crane and began
barking orders. There was very little time to act.
Black vans were coming. That could mean only
one thing: NAARF agents were on the way!

NAARF Attacks!

"Tooth and Clovis, get the little ones to safety in the forest. Take some food with you. We don't know how long you may need to remain in hiding. Kitten, I'll need you to stay and help me here at the barn. It will be perilous, but I can't do it alone," Cletus said.

"Sure, Cletus. Whatever you say. I'm not afraid of any old NAARFers!"

"This is no time to be cocky, young man. These are the most dangerous kind of people," Cletus warned.

Clovis spoke up in a tiny, wavering voice. "I'm not leaving. This is my place now, and they can't make me leave."

"Now Clovis, we've no time for this. Please just go with Tooth," Cletus fussed.

"No, Cletus, she's right," said Tooth. "This is our home, and we're all going to defend it together. Now, what's the plan?" She and Clovis didn't budge.

"Well, all right," said Cletus, seeing that he was outvoted. "First we must erase any clue that we've been in this barn. That means covering up the kitchen and the shop, cutting down the lift, and hiding the vehicles. And I'll rig up a little surprise for our visitors."

Kitten said, "I'll use the Reed Basket to

bulldoze those boxes and cover the doorways."

"Blossom and I will take care of the lift," shouted Beatrice. "When we get through, it'll just look like an old pile of lumber and rope!" She and Blossom raced off toward the loft.

"If only I had dug those escape tunnels. I have the plans, but . . ." Cletus moaned.

"No time for recriminations, Cletus!" shouted Tooth. "Quickly now—tell Clovis and me how we can help."

Cletus glanced about, gathering his wits. "There's a Tesla coil in the loft," he said. "Set it up just out of sight . . . over there. When you feel the barn shake, I want you to flip the switch. Then be sure to stand back!"

Tooth said, "The barn is going to sha . . . ?"

"No time to explain, dear. Hurry!" said Cletus.

Once Cousin Clovis and Tooth were on their way, Cletus pulled the Wicker Crane behind his beloved pile of rejectamenta. He let out the winch cable and wrapped it around one of the barn's support posts.

Cletus tightened the cable as far as it would go and set the brake on the winch. Then he and Kitten covered up the Wicker Crane with a tarp and went to check on the others.

The Peep ran up to Cletus holding a book of matches in his beak.

"Brilliant, Peep, my boy! That's just the ticket. Quickly now, everyone. Up to the loft! As soon as things get going, you know what to do," said Cletus. "Remember, make sure no one sees you!"

Cletus and Kitten hid under the tarp near the winch end of the Wicker Crane. The barn fell silent.

The group heard a grumbling roar outside as the black NAARF vans pulled up and a flurry of agents piled out. Behind them, on leashes, scampered their wily secret weapons.

A low voice called out, "Can't use the infrared here. Targets are too small to show up. But no matter. The weasels will sniff 'em out. Fan out and check the perimeter first . . ."

Kitten whispered, "Cletus, did you hear that? They're using weasels!" He peeked out from under the tarp. Three agents darted past the barn door. "Cletus!"

"*Shhh!* It can't be helped," he said. "We must stick to the plan."

"But I . . ." Kitten stammered.

Cletus gave him a sharp look and Kitten let the tarp fall back into place. In a flash the agents were inside the barn. The weasels strained at their leashes, nosing around at edges and corners.

Moving as quietly as he could, Cletus grabbed the winch handle and began working it back and forth. The line tightened

and tugged at the post, then suddenly went slack. The post rocked and creaked, and the whole barn began to shake.

"Hey!" shouted one of the agents. "The walls are about to give way!"

The building creaked and groaned and vibrated. The NAARF crew scattered. Suddenly a streak of blue light shot out of nowhere and circled about their heads.

"*Yeeow*, what was that? Lightning?"

The weasels slunk down low to the ground, forgetting to sniff and search. A second ball of blue light shot out of the loft, temporarily blinding the agents.

The blast blew Clovis's beret right off her head. She and Tooth watched helplessly as it floated to the ground. They peered nervously over the edge of the loft, certain the beret had given away their position. But in the commotion one of the NAARF agents stepped on it, and the beret disappeared from view.

"Can't be lightning!" the lead agent shouted. "It's not raining."

"Yes, it is! And it's raining in here, too. This place is a deathtrap, sir. Any minute now it's gonna self-destruct.

We've got to . . ." The agent's voice was drowned out by the sounds of water.

Throughout the barn a whizzling, stinging rain was falling. From his hiding place, The Peep had lit up the entire book of matches and was holding them near the sprinkler activation unit. Water came down in all directions, and the NAARF agents panicked. One weasel went wild and bit his handler on the ankle. Another weasel ran for cover under the nearby tarp. There he came face to face with Cletus and Kitten!

"Fall back, fall back!" the lead agent called. "This place is leaking like a sieve. Nothing could live in here." He darted out the door.

Under the tarp the three animals stared at each other. This spy is going to give us away, thought Cletus. Best to save the others.

Cletus was ready to give himself up to the men outside, but Kitten held up his paw. For a long moment, Kitten and the weasel stood eye to eye. Then quite abruptly the weasel scurried off, broke free from his handler, and ran squeaking to each of his companions. At that, every one of the weasels broke leash and ran out of the barn, leaving the NAARF agents in chaos.

A few of the agents raced after the escapees, but the weasels didn't stop until they reached the safety of their old homes, far down the riverbank. The rest of the men ran for the vans. Engines roared and tires screeched as the NAARF crew took off in pursuit of their companions and the runaway weasels. Almost as quickly as it had begun, the crisis at Runt Farm was over.

Cletus and Kitten raced to the top of the hay bales to check on everyone. The Peep had a few singed feathers, but was in good spirits nonetheless. Beatrice and Blossom were huddled under a grandma quilt in the top

bunk. And Tooth and Cousin Clovis stood arm in arm nearby, looking quite bedraggled.

"Everyone all right?" Cletus asked.

"Dear me. That certainly was exciting," Tooth said. "Yes, we appear to be just fine."

"Oh, but look at our dear home," cried Clovis. "It's a mess!"

"No worries, though. We can fix that," said Cletus. "There's just one thing I don't understand." He looked at Kitten. "Why didn't that weasel give us away when he found us under the tarp?"

Beatrice gasped. "Weasel! There was a naarfy *weasel* on you?"

"Well, that's easy to explain," Kitten said. "That guy was sort of a buddy of mine before NAARF caught him. His name is Skeezle. He's kinda slow and the other guys make fun of him. But I was nice to him, so I guess he liked me. He's the one who gave me the cigars." He glanced at Tooth. "And . . . well, he sure wasn't slow today, huh?"

"Uh huh!" said Beatrice.

At that the whole family laughed. Delighted and very much relieved, they clapped each other on the back and hugged. They began trading stories of the fight.

"Did you see that big guy when the light flashed?" Blossom exclaimed. "He jumped so high I was afraid he'd see us up here for sure!"

"Were *you* scared?" Beatrice asked The Peep.

At that The Peep gave his own blow-by-blow description of the day, beginning with the hair-raising kite ride and ending with his rainmaker finale. All listened spellbound. What a day they'd had! The Peep took a bow and everyone applauded.

"Well," said Tooth, shaking her head, "I'm just glad you got the sprinkler started in here when you did. And mind you, young ones, all matches are firmly off limits! Not sure I'd have allowed this plan to go forward if I'd realized . . . Anyway, it's all worked out now, I suppose." She took The Peep's wing tenderly. "I'd better make a poultice for these burns, though."

They were all too tired to clean up the barn.
In fact, it was all they could do to make their
way up the hill to collect the abandoned picnic
and bring it back home. Everyone agreed they
felt a bit safer up in the loft, so that's where
dinner was served. After they ate, Tooth saw to
The Peep's burned feathers and Cletus handed

out grandma quilts.

"G'night, Runt Farmers," said Kitten.

Beatrice and Blossom giggled. "'Night," they said.

"*Peep*," said The Peep.

Cletus's Tesla coil still glowed at the edge of the loft. "Shall I shut this thing off?" he asked.

"Oh, please don't," said Clovis. "It's rather nice. Like a lovely night light."

Soon the family was drifting off to sleep, safe beneath the pulsing blue light that had helped to save them all.

Cletus put his arm around Tooth. She sighed.

"My, but it's nice to have our peace and quiet restored," said Tooth.

"Yes," agreed Cletus. "But now I'll have to think of something new for Halloween."

Glossary

a rexia [a-REX-ee-a]—Beatrice's mispro-
nunciation of the word anorexia—an
eating disorder

beret [bur-AY]—A cap with no brim or bill,
made of soft cloth

bombilatious [BOM-bul-A-shus]—Having the
quality of humming or buzzing

chamomile [KAM-uh-meel]—A plant used to
make a mild tea

chaos [KAY-ahs]—Extreme confusion and
disorder

coefficient [ko-uh-FISH-unt]—A number
expressing the amount of some change or
effect under certain conditions

components [kum-PO-nunts]—Parts

contraption [kun-TRAP-shun]—A device that
is very useful for a particular job

conveyor [kun-VAY-ur]—A long, flat, rotating
belt used to move items

deluded [dee-LOO-dud]—Having a false belief

enlighten [en-LITE-in]—To create
understanding, to clear up or make free
from confusion

evaporate [ee-VAP-ur-ate]—Dry up

extravaganza [ex-tra-vuh-GAN-zuh]—Big, fancy
party or production

flawed [flawd]—Has mistakes or is not perfect

fraudulent [FRA-du-lunt]—Cheating or being
dishonest

girth [gurth]—The distance around a person's body

identity theft [i-DEN-ti-tee theft]—Using someone's personal information to steal from them

infrared [in-fra-RED]—Light waves that can't be seen by human eyes

ingravescent [in-gra-VES-ent]—Growing worse, as in a disease

laboratory [LAB-ra-tor-ee]—A room or building for scientific research and experiments

muse [myooz]—The source of an artist's inspiration

penthouse [PENT-hous]—An apartment located on the top floor of a building

perimeter [pur-IM-it-ur]—The area around the edge of a place

perishable [PARE-ish-a-bul]—Food that will

decay if not kept cold

persona [pur-SONE-uh]—A social role, or a
character played by an actor

provisions [pro-VIZH-uns]—Supplies, like food
and clothing

pseudonym [SUE-du-nim]—A made-up name

recrimination [re-KRIM-in-A-shun]—To accuse
of wrong doing, or to express regret

Tesla coil [TES-la koil]—A high-voltage
electrical transformer named after its
inventor, Nikola Tesla

velvetina [VEL-vu-TEE-nuh] and **wetherwort**
[WE-thur-wort]—Made-up names for
soothing ingredients

vexation [veks-A-shun]—Upset

About the Author

Amanda Lorenzo was born on the West Coast of the United States and has managed to live close to salt water ever since. She shares her home in Seattle, Washington, with her cool cat, Chiti. Amanda loves to sing and has taught music to children ages 5 to 13. She is often surprised by the funny and goofy things that her characters insist on doing, and finds herself laughing even when she knows how the story's going to end.

To invite Amanda Lorenzo to speak to your school
or group, please visit www.RuntFarm.com.

About the Illustrator

Mark Evan Walker lives in the wilds of
suburban Texas, and draws Runt Farm amidst
mighty oaks, magnolias, and brilliantly colored
crepe myrtle and althaeas. Mark would like to
thank all the Runt Farmers for being so kind
as to pose on those occasions when needed to
help tell their stories. He would also like to
thank Cletus for the suggestion about fixing
his drawing board, and Tooth for the delicious
blueberry pie. Yum!

Read a Sneak Preview of Runt Farm: Book 4!

Haunted Runt Farm

Beatrice woke up early. A quiet morning, except . . . the kitchen door was closed, and a thin strip of light peeked out from underneath. A chilly wind whistled through the cracks in the barn walls. Beatrice shivered as she burrowed under the grandma quilt. Then she popped up with a start. The nesting box was rocking back and forth. "Blossom!" she grumbled as the young squirrel turned over in his sleep. Blossom's tail floofed over the side of the bed. Beatrice gave it a yank.

"*Yeeoww!*" Blossom yelled, now wide awake. He swished his tail out of her grasp, then swung over the side to scold his tormentor. "Puh-*leeze*! That is just so *rude!* My tail is *not* a doorbell!"

"Well, you should pay more attention to that bushy thing. It was doing a regular twitchfest all night. Wakes me up on the left side, then on the right side. It's torture, I tell you! "

"What's with all the racket?" said Kitten, giving Beatrice and Blossom a stern look. The Peep paddled up behind Kitten, making his own grumpy face.

"Look, all of you," Beatrice said, pointing at the sliver of light. "Something is up. Cletus and Tooth and Clovis are having some kind of meeting in the kitchen—without us." She crossed her paws and frowned. "It's not fair," she said. "It's . . . it's rude."

"Like pulling a guy's tail?" Blossom shot back. "You're just jealous because your tail's a stumpy bump, and mine's long and luxurious like a stallion's mane."

Kitten cut them off. "Chill, you two. I got more sleeping to do."

"Kitten!" huffed Beatrice, "don't you *care?* Something is going on and they're not even telling us about it. It's like the Mouse Club down there."

"*Peep, peep!*" The Peep added.

"Of course I'm right," Beatrice continued. "It's been like this ever since those NAARF guys and their naarfy weasels showed up here. Early morning meetings with just Cletus, Tooth, and Clovis, and none of *us*. They're cooking up something in that kitchen, and it's not Cheesy Puffers!"

Blossom chimed in, "Yes, that's true . . ." His tail twitched back and forth as he thought it over.

Beatrice pulled the grandma quilt close around her and leaped out of bed. "Well, I for one am going to find out!" she announced, pointing toward the ceiling for dramatic effect.

"Not me," said Kitten, wide-eyed, shaking his head. "If those guys want to talk without us, then let 'em. They're a whole lot smarter than we are. There's a 99 percent chance they know exactly what they're doing." Kitten returned to his favorite spot on the hay bale and curled up on his raggedy-soft blanket. The Peep followed, muttering under his breath.

"See, even The Peep agrees with me!" Beatrice shouted across the loft.

"What should we do?" asked Blossom.

"Snoop, of course," said Beatrice.

In a flash, bunny and squirrel were downstairs. They crouched down and peered under the heavy kitchen door. Through the gap they saw Cletus and Clovis at the table. Tooth brought a pot of tea over from the stove.

"Yes, Cletus," she said, "it's a clever plan, to be sure, but none of us have ever done anything like it before." She clasped her paws. "Dear me, but I do think better with a broom in my hand." Tooth grabbed the straw broom and began sweeping bits of dirt and herbs into a pile. "I'll just sweep this under the door for now."

A cloud of dust shot out from under the door.

"*Fawf!*" coughed Blossom as he tumbled over backward. He sat up, spitting dirt.

"*Arrrrk gak,*" Beatrice scowled, dusting herself off. "This won't work."

"Well," said Blossom, "one thing we do know. Tooth never cleans this hard unless something's bothering her."

"Right," said Beatrice.

Blossom bounded toward the barn door. "Let's try outside by the window! Tooth always leaves it open a bit when she puts the teapot on."

The two crept along the outer wall of the barn. The wind whipped around them, and Beatrice shivered in her quilt. As they made their way, Blossom's tail twitched. With a loud *thump!* it struck the old boards.

"You're doing that thing with your tail again," Beatrice said in a loud whisper.

"I know! I can't help it." Blossom reached over his head and grabbed hold of his tail to keep it quiet. He stepped forward holding his breath, but his tail sprang free just as they arrived under the kitchen window. *Whump!* It whacked the side of the barn. The two of them heard only one word before Tooth's paw came into view. *Bang!* Down went the window.

"Did you hear that?" Blossom whispered.

"Uh huh," said Beatrice. "They said . . . *danger.*"

"We'd better go tell Kitten and The Peep," said Blossom.

"No," said Beatrice. "We're gonna march right in there and find out what's going on!"

To Ruthie

who told me many endearing stories

and listened to mine.

Published by BooktiMookti Press · Seattle, WA · www.booktimookti.com · FIRST EDITION · Book Design by Shannon McCafferty · Library of Congress Cataloging-in-Publication Data · Lorenzo, Amanda · Clovis Escapes! / by Amanda Lorenzo · Illustrations by Mark Evan Walker · Summary: Cousin Clovis comes to live at Runt Farm, and agents of NAARF attack. 1. Animals—Fiction 2. Family—Fiction · I. Walker, Mark Evan ill II. Title III. Series Lorenzo, Amanda Runt Farm Series bk 3 · ISBN 13: 978-0-9800952-2-7

Printed in Stevens Point, WI, USA 10/2009, Batch #200910

BooktiMookti Press is committed to preserving ancient forests and natural resources. We elected to print this title on 30% post consumer recycled paper, processed chlorine free. As a result, for this printing, we have saved three trees, two million BTUs of energy, 224 pounds of CO_2 in greenhouse gases, 1,015 gallons of wastewater, and 118 pounds of solid waste. Environmental impact estimates were made using the Environmental Defense Paper Calculator, *www.papercalculator.org*.